Tog the Sporty Dog

Colin and Jacqui Hawkins

FAMILY LEARNING

Exercise is fun
for everyone!

FAMILY LEARNING

from Dorling Kindersley

The Family Learning mission is to support the concept
of the home as a center of learning and to help families
develop independent learning skills to last a lifetime.

Editors: Bridget Gibbs, Fiona Munro, Constance Robinson
Designers: Chris Fraser, Lisa Hollis

Published by Family Learning

Southland Executive Park, 7800 Southland Boulevard
Orlando, Florida 32809

Dorling Kindersley registered offices:
9 Henrietta Street, Covent Garden, London WC2E 8PS

VISIT US ON THE WORLD WIDE WEB AT:
www.dk.com

ISBN 0-7894-4677-4

Color reproduction by DOT Gradations
Printed in Hong Kong by Wing King Tong

Do you know about Tog?
"I'm a very sporty dog," said Tog.
One day he went out for a jog.

Tog met his friend, Hog.
"Hi, Hog. Come for a jog," said Tog.
"No thanks, Tog. Hogs don't jog like dogs.
We're not fast enough. It's just too tough."
Tog said, "That's not true, jogging's good
for you. Come and run, it's lots of fun!"

"Well, I am a little bit fat," said Hog.
"I'll soon get rid of that," said Tog the dog.
"Come on, let's jog, you lazy Hog."

"You'll need new stuff, you realize, when you start to exercise," said Tog the dog to Hog. At the sports store there was lots to choose. Hog bought himself some running shoes.

Though Tog and Hog weren't tall, Tog wanted Hog to try basketball. "I'm too short for this sport," said Hog, as Tog whizzed around the court.

Tog jogged to the gym and took Hog along with him. Tog trained hard to keep fit. Hog didn't like it one little bit!

"Exercise is great. It keeps
down your weight," said Tog.
"Doing gym is very tough.
I've already had quite enough!"
said Hog to Tog the sporty dog.

"You don't like the gym, so how about a swim? That will make you trim," said Tog. "But the water's chilly," said Hog. "Don't be silly," said Tog.

Then he gave a big grin and pushed Hog in. SPLOSH!

Hog was tired and Hog was hot, but Tog the sporty dog was not.
"1, 2, 3, skip like me!" said Tog with glee.
"I'm wiped out," said Hog.
"That's what getting fit's about!" said Tog.

"Let's go and skate!" said sporty Tog.
"But it's getting late!" said poor tired Hog.
"I'll race you," said Tog and off he flew.
Poor Hog was scared, he couldn't skate
and Tog the dog wouldn't wait!

"I think you'll like tennis," said Tog.
Hog said, "Tog, you're a menace!"
With a WHACK! and a SMACK!
Tog served an ace and hit Hog in the face!

Hog was so upset,
he tied Tog up in the net.
"What a catch!"
said Hog to Tog.
"That's the end of the match!"

"I don't want to be fit or thinner.
I just want my dinner. NOW!" said Hog.
"OK, you win," said Tog, with a grin.
"You've done your best, you need a rest."

"I'm ready to drop. Please, can we stop?" puffed Hog. "Here's just the place to put a smile on your face," said Tog the sporty dog, as they came to a café that was open all day.

"What a treat! What will you eat?" asked Tog. "I'll have soup in a bowl with a big buttered roll. Maybe tuna on rye — no, a chicken pot pie. A pizza with cheese and tomato, please. Then a chocolate cake and a big milkshake," said hungry Hog to Tog the dog.

If Hog eats all that...

...he'll really be fat!

As Tog watched Hog chew and chew, he said "I know just the sport for you! Food's the thing that you like best – this will put you to the test!"

Said Hog to Tog, "What sport can that be?"
But Tog just smiled and said, "Follow me!"

"Here's a clue," Tog said at last.
"There's lots of food,
but you must run fast."

"Hog, grab a pan and run as fast as you can," said Tog. Suddenly it all became clear. "It's a pancake race!" said Hog with a cheer!
"Get ready! Get set!
Go, Hog, Go!" shouted Tog,
"Don't be slow!"

Hog ran so fast he thought he would fly, tossing his pancake high in the sky. He was first over the line, in double-quick time!

"Yum, yum!" said Hog.
"I'm ready to burst!"
"You're the best!" laughed Tog.
"You've come in first!"